JAKE MADDOX

OBSTACLE CHALLENGE

BY JAKE MADDOX

Text by Shawn Pryor

Illustrated by Giuliano Aloisi

STONE ARCH BOOKS
a capstone imprint

Jake Maddox Adventure is published by Stone Arch Books,
an imprint of Capstone.
1710 Roe Crest Drive
North Mankato, Minnesota 56003
www.capstonepub.com

Library of Congress Cataloging-in-Publication Data is available on
the Library of Congress website.

ISBN: 978-1-4965-8696-4 (hardcover)
ISBN: 978-1-4965-9204-0 (paperback)
ISBN: 978-1-4965-8697-1 (eBook PDF)

Summary: Tanisha Carter can't believe her luck when she finds
out her favorite extreme obstacle course challenge is coming to her
town. She needs a partner to compete, so her pal, Derek, agrees
to team up with her. But when training reveals Tanisha's fear
of heights, the pair realizes they have more than one obstacle to
overcome in this extreme challenge.

Designer: Lori Bye

Printed in the United States of America.
PA100

TABLE OF CONTENTS

CHAPTER 1

EXTREME OBSTACLE

In the living room, twelve-year-old Tanisha Carter picked up her controller and settled onto the sofa. She was ready to play one of her favorite online multiplayer games.

But before she could get started, her older brother, Terrell, walked into the living room. He plopped down next to her on the couch.

"Hey, T, how long are you going to play your game?" he asked. "There's a basketball game on in thirty minutes. I was hoping to use the TV so I don't have to watch it on my phone."

"That's just enough time for me to crush three levels," Tanisha said. "The TV is all yours after that."

"Thanks!" said Terrell. "Hey, did you see the new ad for *Rugged Reaper*? They're coming here next month. I know how much you love that show."

Tanisha's eyes opened wide at the mention of her favorite show. "What?" she hollered. "Show it to me NOW!"

Terrell chuckled as he loaded the trailer on his phone. "Chill, sis, OK," he said, handing her the phone.

Tanisha could barely contain her excitement as she pressed play. Her mouth hung open as she watched kids her own age barrel through an intense-looking obstacle course.

"This is awesome!" she said.

"Kids, you think you know what an obstacle course is?" the announcer said.

Tanisha couldn't take her eyes off the screen. Exciting music played as the announcer's voice boomed.

"You've seen nothing until you've challenged the Rugged Reaper," he continued. "The best obstacle course designed for kids, by kids!"

Tanisha was laser focused. She watched *Rugged Reaper* every week. The competitors were fierce.

"The number-one TV show for kids has mud runs, balance beams, rope swings, wall climbing, and the dreaded monkey bars of infinity!" the announcer continued. "And we're coming to your town!"

Tanisha paused the video. "Are they really coming to Newville?" she asked her brother.

Terrell nodded. "I checked the website. We're one of the stops."

Tanisha pressed play again and listened to the rest of the details.

"The top three teams will advance to the national quarterfinals in Orlando, Florida!" the announcer shouted.

"If you're between the ages of eight and twelve and love to have fun while getting dirty, sign your two-person team up for this extreme obstacle course today!" the announcer finished.

Tanisha couldn't believe her luck. "I've always wanted to do this!" she said. "I'm going to get a teammate and sign up tomorrow!"

Terrell gave his younger sister a skeptical look. "I don't know, T. It's one thing to watch it on TV. Do you really think you'd be up for that type of challenge?" he said. "There's no way you can find a teammate and get ready that fast. That's like a month away!"

"I can do anything I set my mind to," Tanisha snapped. "You'll see." She just had to find a teammate.

* * *

At school the next day, Tanisha sat with her friends in the cafeteria. She couldn't stop talking about *Rugged Reaper*.

"All I need is a teammate so we can sign up and start training." Tanisha looked at her friend Justin. "Do you want to join my team?"

"I would," said Justin, taking a sip of his soda. "But it's basketball season. Practice and games take up most of my time."

Tanisha turned to her friend Nicole. "What about you?" she asked. "You're a great gymnast. We'd be unstoppable!"

Nicole made a face as she picked out the peas that had spilled into the dessert on her tray. "Sorry, T," she said. "My gymnastics coach won't let me take on any other extracurricular activities."

Tanisha sighed. "It's OK," she said, even though she was disappointed. "I wouldn't want you to get into trouble."

She pushed her tray to the side and let out a sigh. *If none of my friends can do the Rugged Reaper with me, then what am I going to do?*

Just then Derek Reeves approached their table. "Hey, guys, is it cool if I sit with you?" he asked, holding his tray of food.

"Yeah, have a seat," Justin replied. "There's always room for one more."

"What's new?" Derek asked, contemplating the mystery meat in his sandwich.

"T is trying to recruit a teammate so she can compete on *Rugged Reaper*," Nicole said. "Justin and I are both too busy, though."

"*Rugged Reaper*? It's coming here? When?" Derek said, putting down his sandwich. "I'm obsessed with that show. I watch it on the Travel Games Channel all the time. It looks so fun!"

Tanisha shot Derek a thoughtful look. "In May," she said. "My brother just showed me the ad yesterday." She paused. "Would you want to be my teammate?"

Tanisha's friends seemed stunned.

"You think Derek would be good on an obstacle course?" Justin said. He shot the other boy a look. "No offense, man. It just doesn't seem like the type of thing you'd be into."

Unlike Justin, Derek wasn't on the basketball team and didn't seem to care about sports in general. He always seemed a little out of shape in gym class. But he was one of the nicest kids at school.

"Cause I'm a little bigger? I might not be as athletic as you," Derek said, "but I'm strong."

"Derek did save our butts in tug-of-war against Mr. Drexel's class," Nicole added.

"That's right! With your strength and my speed, we'd make a great team!" Tanisha exclaimed. "Not to mention how much we know about the show. So you'll do it? You'll be my teammate?"

"Sure!" Derek said, giving Tanisha a high five.

CHAPTER 2

IN TRAINING

Derek and Tanisha walked home together after school that day, planning out the next month before the big day.

"We need to get started with our training ASAP," Tanisha said.

"How do we do that?" Derek asked. "We can't tear up our parents' backyards to build a practice course, and the school playground isn't enough."

"Well, we have to do something so we don't embarrass ourselves," Tanisha said.

Suddenly Derek stopped in his tracks and smiled. "Janet!" he exclaimed.

"Janet?" Tanisha repeated. She raised her eyebrow in confusion.

"My cousin Janet runs a gym," Derek explained. "I don't know why I didn't think of it sooner."

"Do you think she'd let us train there?" Tanisha asked.

"Worth a try. Let's stop there tomorrow after school and ask," he said.

"OK," Tanisha said, crossing her fingers. "Hopefully it'll work out. No pun intended!"

* * *

The next day after school, Tanisha and Derek went to Janet's gym, EveryFit. They opened the double doors to the gym, looking on in awe.

"This place is huge!" Tanisha exclaimed.

Janet exited her office and walked over to Derek and Tanisha. "Hey, Derek," she said, giving him a hug. "Your mom told me you'd be stopping by with a friend of yours."

"Hi, cuz," Derek replied. "This is my friend Tanisha from school. We're signing up to compete on *Rugged Reaper* next month and need a place to train. Any chance we can do it here?"

Janet thought for a moment. "I don't see why not," she said.

"Awesome!" Tanisha and Derek hollered, high-fiving each other.

Janet held up a hand. "Two conditions, though," she said. "First, you help at the gym a couple hours a week. Second, you let me train you."

Derek and Tanisha looked at each other and turned to Janet. "Deal!" they said in unison.

"Where do we start?" Derek asked. "How about the climbing wall over there? I know there's one in the Rugged Reaper course. That would help us practice."

Tanisha felt uneasy looking at the massive climbing wall. It was more than twenty feet high. She was overwhelmed by its height.

"Maybe we shouldn't start with the hard stuff today," she said. She pointed to the rowing machines. "Those look cool."

Janet shook her head. "You're doing an obstacle course with a lot of running and endurance activities," she said. "Let's start with cardio and circuit training. Go to the locker rooms and change into your workout clothes, then meet me in the training area."

Tanisha and Derek did as they were told. Minutes later, they were standing with Janet at one of the training areas.

"All right, let's warm up and stretch a bit, and then we'll get started," Janet said. "Warming up and stretching improves your heart rate and prevents fatigue. It also minimizes your risk of pulling or straining a muscle."

Janet showed Tanisha and Derek how to properly stretch their calves, hips, arms, necks, legs, and shoulders. Then they were ready to begin.

"Let's start a cycle of twenty push-ups, sit-ups, and jumping jacks," Janet said. "Go!"

Derek and Tanisha had no problems doing the push-ups. But as Tanisha blazed through her sit-ups and began her jumping jacks, Derek struggled.

After finishing her jumping jacks, Tanisha looked at Derek. "C'mon, Derek, you can do it," she said. "Only four more to go! You've got this!"

Derek completed his sit-ups and quickly did his jumping jacks. After finishing, he was breathing heavily.

"Sorry, T," Derek said, panting. "I don't want to slow us down. I've never been good at sit-ups."

"It's OK. It's our first day. The more we train, the better we'll get!" Tanisha said, trying to sound positive. "We just have to support each other."

"She's right," Janet agreed, nodding. "Having a supportive partner makes a difference. But so does training, so let's get back to work! Another round of push-ups, sit-ups, and jumping jacks. Go!"

After completing a few sets, Janet led them over to the balance beam next. It looked just like the one on *Rugged Reaper*.

"You'll need some balance training," Janet told the kids. "Climb up on the beam and slowly walk across. Focus on your center of gravity and posture. The more you practice, the quicker you'll be able to go."

Derek got on the beam first. After a few steps, he lost his balance and fell off the beam. He landed on the mat below with a *thud*!

"Oof!" Derek coughed.

Tanisha stepped onto the beam next. She was halfway across and feeling good, so she decided to pick up the pace. Almost immediately she lost her balance and fell on the mat.

"Ow," she muttered. "This place needs softer mats."

"What did I say before you got on the beam?" Janet asked.

"Slowly walk across the beam, and the more we practice, the better we'll get," Tanisha said.

Janet nodded. "That's right. Now both of you get back on the beam and try again."

CHAPTER 3

A TALL PROBLEM

Tanisha and Derek continued training with Janet at the gym every day after school. That weekend, they helped at the gym as repayment. After a week of training, they were already starting to see some improvement.

"I can actually run a couple laps around the track without getting tired or taking a break," Derek said. "I've never been able to do that before!"

"I know!" Tanisha agreed. "And your cousin's nutrition tips have been a big help. I've been drinking more water and less soda and not eating as much junk food. I don't feel as sluggish as I did last week."

"We're going to do great on *Rugged Reaper*!" Derek said.

"Bring it on!" Tanisha agreed.

Janet approached the kids. "Looks like you two are all ready for training today," she said.

"Definitely," Tanisha agreed. "And we got an e-mail with additional rules about the course. You can help your partner on the terror wall and infinity monkey bars."

"But if one of the players falls off an obstacle, he or she has to start the obstacle all over again," Derek added.

Janet walked the kids over to the gym's climbing wall. "Speaking of walls, I think today is the right time for both of you to practice some climbing."

Tanisha and Derek looked up at the climbing wall in front of them. It stretched all the way to the ceiling.

"Whoa," Tanisha said. The wall seemed even higher than she remembered.

Janet helped both Tanisha and Derek with their climbing harnesses. Then she secured their bungee ropes.

"When climbing, remember that your legs are stronger than your arms," she told them. "So focus on your foot and leg placement. And take your time today. This is new for both of you."

Derek approached the wall first. "I've got this," he said under his breath.

Tanisha watched as Derek started to climb. She froze where she stood as she realized how tall the wall was.

"Tanisha, are you going to start climbing?" Janet asked.

Tanisha gulped nervously. "Um, yeah," she said. "I was just watching how well Derek is doing. I'll get started."

Derek was already near the top of the wall as Tanisha began.

"I can do this. I can do this," Tanisha repeated to herself. She placed her foot on the first foothold.

As Tanisha neared the halfway mark on the wall, she paused. Looking up, she saw Derek start to make his descent back down. Then she looked down. Janet looked like a tiny speck down below.

Tanisha started to sweat. Her fingers tingled. She'd never been up this high before.

"Hey, T, are you OK?" Derek asked, pausing near her. He looked concerned.

Tanisha sweated even more. "Um, I'm not feeling so well all of a sudden. I'm sorry."

"It's all right," Derek said. "Do you want me to help you down?"

"No, no, it's OK," she said. "Just give me a few minutes. I'll get down."

Tanisha wheezed. Only halfway up the wall, and she felt as if she couldn't breathe, let alone move. If she looked up, the wall seemed even more terrifying. If she looked down, she felt like she was going to puke.

She'd never felt this way before, but it suddenly hit her—she was afraid of heights. And if she couldn't conquer her fear, she'd embarrass herself on television—and let down her teammate.

CHAPTER 4

FEAR

Later that week, Tanisha was sitting at the kitchen table, doing her homework, when Terrell walked in.

"Hey, T," he said. He headed to the fridge to grab a drink. "*Rugged Reaper* is on. You want to watch?"

"That's OK," Tanisha said, looking through her textbook.

"But you never miss an episode," Terrell replied. "I'm sure Mom and Dad won't mind if you finish—"

"I said I don't want to watch it!" Tanisha snapped.

Terrell looked shocked. "Geez. What's your problem?" he said.

"It's nothing," Tanisha said, shaking her head.

Terrell pushed Tanisha's textbook away and sat next to her at the table. "C'mon, what's wrong?"

Tanisha sighed. "Derek and I were training earlier this week, and I froze on the climbing wall. Apparently I'm afraid of heights. Now I don't know if I can do this. Maybe you were right. Maybe I can't do the Rugged Reaper after all."

Terrell shook his head. "I was just giving you a hard time. You and Derek have been working too hard on this for you to quit."

"But what if I mess up? I'll be letting Derek down too," Tanisha replied.

"You'll never know unless you try. And I believe in you. You should talk to your trainer or Derek about this. Maybe they can help," Terrell said.

* * *

Tanisha got to her next training session early, in the hopes of shaking her fear. She put on her climbing harnesses and secured her bungee rope. Looking up at the wall, she began to climb.

But after only three small levels, Tanisha's heart began to pound. She looked up at the top of the wall and began to sweat heavily. She was afraid to climb any higher.

Tanisha quickly got down off the wall, removing the bungee rope and harness.

What am I going to do? she worried.

A moment later, Derek walked up. "Hey, T!" he called. "I got here early to do some pull-ups before we started training. I can do twenty in a row before I get tired!" To prove his point, he picked Tanisha up off the ground.

"OK, OK, I get it!" Tanisha laughed as Derek put her back down.

Just then, Janet walked over. She put them to work right away with a set of push-ups.

"Great job!" Janet said as they finished. "You guys are blazing through those!"

"I'm still too slow with my sit-ups, though," Derek complained.

"But you're great with jumping jacks," Tanisha reminded him. "And you've improved on the balance beam in the past week."

"You're both doing well," Janet agreed. "I think it's time to make it a little tougher." She put ankle weights on both Derek and Tanisha.

"What are these for?" Derek asked. "Isn't running already hard enough?"

"It's going to be even harder in the mud," Janet replied. "These will help prepare you."

Derek started jogging around the gym. "They feel fun—" He suddenly lost his balance and fell to the floor.

Tanisha rushed toward Derek. "Are you all right—" she began. But then she wiped out too, landing on top of Derek. They both laughed.

Janet helped both kids climb to their feet. "They'll also help you with your balance," she told them with a laugh. "Now, I want both of you to walk around the track a few times. Don't run. I don't want you hurting yourselves."

Derek and Tanisha began to walk the track. "Hey, T?" Derek said as they started their first lap.

"What's up?" Tanisha asked.

"I just wanted to say thanks for asking me to be your teammate," Derek said. "I know I wasn't your first choice. And I'm not the most athletic. But you've been a great friend through all of this. I'm really excited for the competition."

"You're welcome," said Tanisha. "This has been a lot of fun, for sure."

But memories of being stuck on the wall—too scared to climb—began to creep in again.

"Hey, can I tell you something?" she asked.

"Sure," Derek nodded. "What is it?"

Tanisha opened her mouth to tell Derek about her fear, but something stopped her. She shouldn't be afraid. Not of something as silly as heights.

Plus, she was the athlete on the team. If Derek, who'd been in worse shape to start, was doing so well, she couldn't let her friend and teammate down. The last thing she wanted was for him to have to worry about her too.

Derek has his own stuff to worry about, Tanisha thought. *I'm going to have to conquer my fear on my own.*

"Eh, it's no big deal," she said. "I'll tell you some other time. Let's see if Janet will let us do monkey-bar training and belly-crawl drills after we walk laps."

CHAPTER 5

HIDING SOMETHING

After weeks of training, it was time for Derek and Tanisha's final session at the gym.

"So, what's the plan for today?" Derek asked Janet.

"Maybe some push-ups and sit-ups, followed by some crawling drills?" asked Tanisha.

Janet handed them each a package. "Not today. The two of you have trained enough. You're ready. Here's a gift for both of you for all of your hard work."

"Cool, thanks, cuz!" Derek said as they opened their gifts. Inside each was a red T-shirt and matching shorts that said *EveryFit Champions*.

"Now you'll be the best-looking team out there," Janet said, smiling. "Your event is in two days, so I want both of you to eat proper meals—no junk food. Drink plenty of water, stay away from distractions and video games, and get a good night's sleep."

"Will do," Tanisha promised.

"I told both of your parents that tonight would be short, so they're waiting for you outside. Good luck. No matter what happens, I'm proud of you both."

Derek gave Janet a big hug. "I really appreciate that, cuz," he said. Turning to Tanisha, he added, "I'll see you at school tomorrow, T!"

"See ya!" said Tanisha. After Derek left, she sighed, lowering her head.

"Hey, what's wrong?" Janet asked.

Tanisha tried to brush it off. "Nothing. Why would you say that?"

"I can see it on your face," Janet replied. "What's bothering you?"

Tanisha let out a big sigh. "It's . . . the climbing wall. I-I-I'm afraid of heights," she managed to get out. "I didn't realize it before we started training, but the wall is so tall, and it freaks me out. I'll be the reason we lose *Rugged Reaper*."

"Why didn't you say something about this sooner?" Janet asked, looking concerned.

Embarrassed, Tanisha looked down at her feet. "I don't know. It's just . . . I didn't want to admit I was afraid," she said. "I didn't want to let Derek down. I'm supposed to be the athlete."

"You're *supposed* to be a team," Janet replied.

"I know," Tanisha said. "And now when we reach the wall I'm going to freak out and not be able to do it."

Janet put her arm around Tanisha's shoulders. "You know, it's OK to be scared, Tanisha," she said. "We all get scared about certain things. When I was your age, I was terrified of the water."

"Water?" Tanisha repeated. She was confused. "Why?"

"I thought I would drown," Janet replied. "I wouldn't go near a swimming pool or beach for a long time. It wasn't until I decided to face my fear that I was able to overcome it. I didn't do it alone. But I did it. And you can too."

Tanisha nodded skeptically. She wanted to believe Janet, but . . .

"Is it OK if I tell my mom to wait a bit? Do you have time to help me on the climbing wall?" she asked.

"Sure thing," said Janet. "We'll get through it together."

Tanisha went to tell her mom she needed more time. When she returned, Janet was at the climbing wall putting on her equipment. Tanisha got into her harness too.

"When we start climbing I want you to focus on your hands, feet, and the wall in front of you," Janet said. "Focus on those three things and don't look up."

"But what if I get—" Tanisha started to say.

Janet read her mind. "If you get scared, close your eyes, take a deep breath, exhale, and calm yourself. Then continue to move up the wall and focus on those three things," she said.

Tanisha nodded and took a deep breath. She began to climb slowly, with Janet climbing right next to her. At first it was slow going, but about halfway up the wall, Tanisha began to move a little faster.

"You're doing it!" Janet yelled.

Tanisha smiled as she looked at Janet. But then she looked upward. Her fear of heights came rushing back.

"I'm right here with you, Tanisha," Janet said. "Don't panic. Remember what I told you to do if you get scared."

Tanisha stopped looking up, looked at Janet, and then closed her eyes. She took a deep breath, exhaled, and looked directly at the wall. She began climbing again.

Tanisha and Janet finished climbing the wall, then made their way back down. At the bottom, Tanisha gave Janet a big hug.

"It was scary, but I did it," Tanisha said. "Will you climb the wall with me again?"

"I'd be glad to," Janet replied.

CHAPTER 6

THE RUGGED REAPER

The big day had finally arrived. Derek and Tanisha met up at the Newville Fields Park and Reserve early that morning. Before long, the stands were filled with *Rugged Reaper* fans, along with the families and friends of the contestants.

Derek and Tanisha took their places at the starting line. The rest of the contestants lined up as well.

"Can you believe the turnout? There must be hundreds of kids waiting to take this course on!" said an excited Derek.

"I had no idea it would be *this* big," Tanisha said. "Look at all the TV cameras. This is wild!"

Just then a couple contestants walked up to Tanisha and Derek. "Hi, I'm Blake," one of the boys said. "This is my friend, Austin."

"I'm Derek, and this is Tanisha," Derek replied. "Nice to meet you both!"

"Is this your first extreme obstacle course?" Blake asked.

Tanisha nodded. "How about you guys?"

"This is our third," Austin replied. "When we found out that *Rugged Reaper* was coming here, we couldn't miss it."

"Any advice you can give us?" Derek asked.

"Accept that you're going to get dirty immediately!" joked Blake.

"And never leave your teammate behind," Austin added.

Just then the announcer made her way to the podium. "Greetings, and welcome to *Rugged Reaper*! Are you all ready?"

The kids all screamed, "Yeah!" in unison.

"Good! Now, because the top three teams will advance to the national quarterfinals, we've made this course extra challenging. There's a special, never-before-seen final obstacle!" the announcer bellowed. "When the pistol fires, begin! Good luck!"

The starter pistol blared, and the kids ran to the first obstacle, the massive mud run. Tanisha and Derek took off through the quarter-mile of mud, dodging the dirt the other kids were splashing up as they ran.

A few kids fell face-first into the mud, causing a chain reaction. Even some of the cameramen got caught up in it. Staying upright, Derek passed them by, followed by Tanisha.

"Janet was smart to make us use those ankle weights!" Tanisha yelled.

"Definitely!" Derek hollered back. "We're almost out of the mud!"

The two finished the mud run and ran quickly to the second obstacle, the baited belly crawl. It was a forty-yard ground crawl under a net.

Tanisha and Derek wiggled under the net and started crawling. Just in front of them, some kids got tangled in the net, slowing them down.

Maneuvering past them, Tanisha crawled quickly on the ground like a mini-locomotive. Derek trailed behind her.

"The net up ahead is hanging low, so don't get tangled, Derek!" Tanisha warned.

"Gotcha. Thanks, partner!" Derek said.

After what seemed like an eternity, Derek and Tanisha exited from the belly crawl. They ran with the other kids to the third obstacle, the sit-up situation station. There were adults stationed there to make sure each teammate did fifty sit-ups.

Tanisha and Derek got to their station and started their repetitions. Tanisha flew through her fifty sit-ups. When she finished, Derek still had twenty-five more to go.

Tanisha got up and cheered her teammate on. "Come on, Derek! You can do it!"

Tanisha was really impressed with how far Derek had come. He finished his sit-ups, and they began running again.

"We've got a half-mile run until our next station," Tanisha said. "Let's go!"

CHAPTER 7

BALANCE, SWING, AND HOLD ON!

Nearing the completion of the half-mile run, Tanisha and Derek were in second place. They were making great time on the course so far.

Around the bend was a volunteer water station to make sure the contestants stayed hydrated. As they ran toward the station, Tanisha saw a familiar face standing there, holding cups of water.

"Terrell?" she exclaimed. "What are you doing here?"

"Trying to be supportive," her brother said, handing her a cup. "Now, don't get distracted by me. Go, go, go!"

Derek and Tanisha both gulped some water and kept running. Soon they arrived at the next obstacle station, the stability beam and swing. It had sets of extended balance beams and a rope swing at the end. A pool of water had been set up underneath the whole obstacle.

"The first-place team is only halfway across the beams. We'll catch up with them for sure!" said Derek.

Tanisha began to make her way slowly along the balance beam. Behind her, the other teams were starting to catch up and test their skills on the beam. Most of the kids went too fast and fell in the water, meaning they had to start all over at the beginning of the beam.

Tanisha was almost to the end of the balance beam. She grabbed the rope to swing toward dry land when she heard . . . *SPLASH!*

Derek had fallen into the water right before reaching the end of the balance beam. He now had to go back to the beginning of the beam and start all over.

"Oh no!" Tanisha cried out after landing on the ground. The teams behind her raced to the next station, putting Tanisha and Derek out of second place.

"I'm sorry, T!" Derek shouted. He crossed the beam again, making it to the end this time and grabbing the rope. He swung to dry land and landed next to Tanisha. "I've messed up everything!"

"No, you haven't. Stop beating yourself up, and let's move!" Tanisha yelled as they raced to the next station, the push-ups of doom.

Each team member had to do one hundred push-ups before being allowed to move forward. Most of the teams were struggling. Everyone was exhausted from the course.

Tanisha grinned. This was the perfect opportunity to catch back up.

An adult watched as they each did one hundred push-ups and were cleared to go to the next station. Their training was paying off!

"We're not too far from the fourth-place team. We still have a chance!" Tanisha said as she and Derek ran down the trail.

"Get ready for the infinity monkey bars!" Derek warned.

Derek started on the monkey bars. Tanisha was right behind him. Halfway through, she started to tire. She tried desperately to hold on.

Like the balance beams, if a contestant fell before completing the bars, he or she had to start all over. Instead of a pool of water below, however, it was a pond of mud.

"All those push-ups wore my arms out," Tanisha said, panting. "I'm having trouble holding on—"

Suddenly she lost her grip. Tanisha fell, waiting to hear the splash of the mud before her. Instead, she was hanging in midair.

Derek was clinging to the monkey bars with one hand. He'd used his other hand to save Tanisha from falling!

"You didn't quit on me when I fell, and I'm not quitting on you!" Derek said.

One of the cameramen moved closer to Derek and Tanisha, capturing the moment. Derek rocked Tanisha back and forth until she could reach the monkey bars. Together, they finished making their way across.

On the sidelines, a judge said, "Teammates can prevent their partner from falling, so she's clear!"

Derek and Tanisha smiled. Then Derek said, "Take a quick breather, T, and let's keep going!"

CHAPTER 8

THE WALL

Derek and Tanisha ran up the trail to the next obstacle, the rock-with-you wall.

Tanisha was shocked to see a very short version of the wall she and Derek had climbed at EveryFit during their training sessions.

"That's it?" she cried. "That's the wall? That's a breeze! We'll be caught up to the third-place team in no time!"

Together, Derek and Tanisha quickly scaled the wall. They jumped off onto a massive, cushioned landing pad.

"I see the third-place team, they're not too far ahead!" Derek yelled. "We can catch up to them on the trail!"

They took off running down the trail, and soon they were within reach of the third-place team. But then they went around the bend to the final obstacle. All the teams paused and stood in awe of the mother wall, a forty-foot-tall, forward-leaning wall.

Tanisha gulped. She stood there, frozen with fear, as the other teams grabbed ropes and started pulling themselves up the wall.

Derek grabbed a rope too and was about to climb when he realized that Tanisha hadn't moved. "T, are you OK?" he called.

"I can't do it, Derek!" Tanisha screamed to her partner. "I'm afraid of heights. That wall is just too tall!"

"I'm scared of this wall too!" Derek shouted back.

"What are you talking about? You had no problem climbing that big wall at the gym!" Tanisha said.

"Yeah, because I was trying to hurry up and get it over with," Derek explained. "I've been intimidated this whole competition. But we've worked hard to get here, and we still have a chance to get third place. The other teams are struggling! Win or lose, we do it together."

Tanisha shook her head and stared up at the wall. It loomed high above her. But then she remembered what Janet had taught her in the gym.

"You're right," Tanisha finally replied. "I might be scared, but let's do this!"

Derek and Tanisha both grabbed a rope and began making their way up the wall. Tanisha's nerves were getting the best of her, but she tried to focus on the wall, her hands, and her feet as she climbed upward. Derek cheered her on as they climbed.

"I'm right here with you!" he called.

Finally they both made it to the top of the wall and looked back down at the wall behind them. They'd come a long way. On the other side, the third-place team had just landed.

Tanisha and Derek nodded at each other, then held each other's hand as they climbed over the top and jumped down. They landed, screaming, on the pad below.

"We did it!" Tanisha cheered. "I can't believe it!"

"It's not over yet! We've got a half-mile run to go," Derek said. "Let's catch up to the other teams and win this thing!"

CHAPTER 9

THE FINAL STRETCH

Tanisha and Derek continued down the trail, getting closer and closer to the third-place team. They were both still holding out hope that they would qualify for the finals on *Rugged Reaper.*

"This half-mile seems like forever!" said Tanisha.

The first- and second-place teams were so far ahead that Derek and Tanisha couldn't see them. But as they approached the dip in the trail, the third-place team tripped!

"We can pass them!" said Derek.

The third-place team quickly got up off the ground. But Tanisha and Derek were right beside them!

There were cameras everywhere. Tanisha could see a ton of them at the finish line up ahead.

"Look! There's the finish line!" Tanisha shouted as they ran side-by-side. "We can do this!"

The final sprint felt like a lifetime. All four kids ran as fast as they could toward the finish! Tanisha's heart was racing as she breathed heavily. Beside her, Derek was panting for air.

"We're almost there!" said Tanisha.

With a sudden flash, they crossed the finish line! They'd done it! They'd completed the Rugged Reaper!

"Did we do it? Did we get third place?" Tanisha asked.

"I don't know," said Derek, gasping for breath. "It was so close. We were right beside them as we crossed the line."

The four kids stood over on the sidelines, waiting to hear who would take third place.

"You two are really good," said one of the kids on the other team. "How many of these obstacle courses have you tried?"

"This is our first," replied Tanisha.

"Really?" the other kid said. "Sure doesn't seem like it!"

Just then, the announcer's voice came over the loudspeaker. "That was a photo finish for third place, folks! Who's ready to hear who made it to the finals?"

The crowd cheered, and Derek grabbed Tanisha's hand.

"Good luck," Tanisha said, crossing her fingers.

"All four of our contestants did great," the announcer continued, "but today, Tony and Billie crossed the line first. They advance to the finals!"

Next to Derek and Tanisha, the other team cheered. Disappointed, Tanisha and Derek shook their hands.

"Congrats," Derek said.

"Thanks!" the other kids said. "Hope to see you at another event!" They walked away to collect their third-place medals.

Tanisha was upset. "I'm sorry, Derek. My fear of heights at the mother wall put us behind. That's why we lost."

"That's not true," Derek said. "I fell on the balance beam. We both made mistakes. But together we beat our fears and did something a lot of first-timers could never do! We came this close to going to the finals! How awesome is that?"

"You're right!" Tanisha said, smiling. "We should be proud of ourselves!"

Derek gave Tanisha a hug. "You're a great teammate and friend, T," he said.

"You too," said Tanisha.

A moment later, Derek and Tanisha's friends and families came over. Everyone was eager to congratulate them.

"I can't believe how well you two did!" said Terrell.

"Not bad for a girl, huh?" Tanisha joked. She looked to Janet. "Is it OK if I come by on Monday to train?"

"Me too!" said Derek. "We're a team!"

"But the event is over," Janet said. "You completed the course."

"We want to be ready for next year!" said Tanisha.

"Yeah!" cheered Derek, fist-bumping Tanisha. "Let's do it!"

AUTHOR BIO

Shawn Pryor is the creator and co-writer of the all-ages graphic novel mystery series Cash & Carrie, writer of *Kentucky Kaiju*, and writer and co-creator of the 2019 GLYPH-nominated football/drama series Force. He is also the author of the Jake Maddox Sports Stories title *Diamond Double Play*. In his free time, Shawn enjoys reading, cooking, listening to music, and talking about why Zack from the *Mighty Morphin Power Rangers* is the greatest superhero of all time.

ILLUSTRATOR BIO

After graduating from the Institute for Cinema and Television in Rome, Italy, in 1995, Giuliano Aloisi began working as an animator, layout artist, and storyboard artist on several TV series and TV games for RAI TV. He went on to illustrate for the comic magazine *Lupo Alberto* and for *Cuore*, a satirical weekly magazine. Giuliano continues to work as an animator and illustrator for advertising companies and educational publishing.

GLOSSARY

center of gravity (SEN-ter uhv GRAV it tee)—the point at which the entire weight of something can be balanced

circuit training (SUR-kit TRAY-ning)—a workout technique involving a series of exercises performed in a rotation with minimal rest, often using different pieces of equipment

competitor (kuhm-PE-tuh-tuhr)—a person who tries to win a race or contest

descent (di-SENT)—moving from a higher to a lower place

endurance (en-DUR-enss)—the ability to keep doing an activity for long periods of time

fatigue (fuh-TEEG)—great tiredness

hydrated (HYE-dray-tid)—having achieved a healthy balance of fluids in the body

massive (MAS-iv)—very large, heavy, and solid

nutrition (noo-TRISH-uhn)—the study of how bodies use food to stay strong and healthy

obstacle (OB-stuh-kuhl)—an object that you have to go around or over; something that blocks your path

overwhelmed (oh-ver-WELMD)—completely overcome by thoughts or feelings

posture (POSS-chur)—the position of your body

skeptical (SKEP-tuh-kuhl)—to doubt that something is true

sluggish (SLUGH-ish)—slow in movement or reaction

unison (YOO-nuh-suhn)—in exact agreement or at the same time

DISCUSSION QUESTIONS

1. Imagine that *Rugged Reaper* is coming to your town and you are selected to compete. Who would you choose to be your partner and why? Talk about what qualities would make that person a great teammate for the obstacle course.

2. Tanisha and Derek spent weeks training and exercising in order to take on the extreme obstacle course. What kind of exercises would you do to prepare for an obstacle course?

3. Tanisha doesn't want to share her fear of heights with Derek because she doesn't want to let him down. Do you think that was a fair reaction? Talk about some other ways she could have handled the situation differently.

WRITING PROMPTS

1. Imagine you've been given the task of creating an obstacle course for your classmates and friends. What kind of obstacles would you have on your course? Draw a map and write a few paragraphs explaining your obstacles and course.

2. It can be interesting to think about a story from a different point of view. Try writing Chapter 7 from Derek's point of view. What do you think was going through his mind when he fell off the balance beam and into the water?

3. Tanisha discovers that she has a fear of heights when she starts training. Have you ever had a fear of heights or something else that you conquered? Write two or three paragraphs about what your fear was and how you overcame it.

MORE ABOUT EXTREME OBSTACLE COURSES

Extreme obstacle courses have grown popular in recent years. In 2017, more than six million people signed up to participate in obstacle courses worldwide. Obstacle course running has become so popular that colleges have even launched organizations and club teams that feature obstacle course training.

One of the toughest obstacle courses of all time is the World's Toughest Mudder. Unlike other obstacle courses, this course runs for twenty-four hours straight! The course can be as short as five miles or as long as twelve miles. But all contestants must loop the course continuously until the clock runs out.

In order to qualify for the World's Toughest Mudder, a contestant must first be one of the finalists in a regular Tough Mudder race. All obstacles for the Tough Mudder are kept secret until the day of the event. That way no one knows what they're preparing for—the whole course is a surprise for everyone who runs it.

On average, only ten percent (or fewer) of the World's Toughest Mudder contestants actually complete the challenge.

ONE OF THE EARLIEST OBSTACLE COURSES IN HISTORY

One of the earliest obstacle-based competitions happened during the 1900 Summer Olympic Games in Paris, France, during the two-hundred-meter obstacle swim.

This wasn't your typical swimming event—it featured three types of obstacles that swimmers had to face in the water:

1. A pole that every swimmer had to climb over

2. A set of rowboats that swimmers had to climb over

3. A set of rowboats that swimmers were forced to swim under

The event was held over a span of two days, with Frederick Lane of Austria winning the gold medal.